THE DRAGONSITTER'S island

Text copyright © 2014 by Josh Lacey
Illustrations copyright © 2014 by Garry Parsons
Text in excerpt from *The Dragonsitter's Party* copyright © 2015 by Josh Lacey
Illustrations in excerpt from *The Dragonsitter's Party* copyright © 2015 by Garry Parsons

Little, Brown and Company

Hachette Book Group
1290 Avenue of the Americas, New York, NY 10104
Visit us at lb-kids.com

Little, Brown and Company is a division of Hachette Book Group, Inc.
The Little, Brown name and logo are trademarks of Hachette Book Group, Inc.

The publisher is not responsible for websites (or their content) that are not owned by the publisher.

First U.S. Hardcover Edition: October 2016
First U.S. Paperback Edition: October 2016
Originally published in Great Britain in 2014 by Andersen Press Limited

Library of Congress Control Number: 2015917040

ISBN 978-0-316-38241-0 (hc)—ISBN 978-0-316-29908-4 (pb)

10 9 8 7 6 5 4 3 2 1

LSC-C

Printed in the United States of America

THE DRAGONSITTER'S Island

Josh Lacey

Illustrated by Garry Parsons

LITTLE, BROWN AND COMPANY
New York • Boston

Dear Uncle Morton,

Where is the key to your house?

We arrived on your island this morning, but we couldn't get in.

Mom thought you might have left it under a stone or buried in a flowerpot, so we searched everywhere.

Emily discovered a silver necklace and I found two coins, but there was no sign of the key.

Through the window I could see your dragons going crazy. I didn't know if they were happy to see us or just hungry, but Arthur was charging around and around the house, knocking over your furniture, and Ziggy wouldn't stop breathing fire.

Luckily, Mr. McDougall was still here. He was sure you wouldn't mind if he broke a window.

Unfortunately, he couldn't open the front door from the inside, so we had to push the suitcases through the window and climb in after them.

Ziggy and Arthur are much happier now that we've given them our presents (a big box of malted milk balls for her and three packets of chocolate mini eggs for him).

They also ate our leftover sandwiches from the train and the book I was reading. Luckily, the book wasn't very good.

Emily and I are going to search your house for the key. Mom says if we can't find it, we'll have to go home tomorrow and the dragons can fend for themselves.

I said I wouldn't mind climbing in and out of the window for the whole week, but Mom told me not to be ridiculous.

Have you taken it by mistake? Didn't you leave a spare anywhere?

Love from your favorite nephew,

Eddie

Dear Uncle Morton,

We haven't found the key, but I have found your phone. Mom called you to leave another message, and I heard it ringing behind the sofa.

I hope you don't need it in Outer Mongolia. I put it on the mantelpiece with the necklace and the coins.

Mr. McDougall has gone back to the mainland in his boat. Emily says it's creepy being the only people here, but I like it.

Thanks for your instructions and the map. Emily and Mom took hours unpacking their bags, so I've been exploring. I climbed Dead Man's

Cairn and walked all the way along the beach to Lookout Point.

Arthur sat on my shoulder like a parrot. At first I was worried he might burn my ear off, but he hasn't been breathing any fire at all. Isn't he old enough?

Eddie

Dear Uncle Morton,

We have now searched your house, your garden, and quite a lot of your island, but we still can't find the key. Please write back ASAP and tell us where it is.

Mom is dead serious about leaving tomorrow. It's not just because of the key. It's the poop, too.

Ziggy did one in the kitchen and another by the back door.

I know it's not her fault. She can't fit through the window, and she has to go somewhere. I just wish she could hold them in until we've found the key.

Also Mom is asking where the can opener is.

We brought some food, but not enough because you told us your cupboard was full of provisions. Unfortunately, all the provisions are in cans.

I'm sure I could open them with a knife, but Mom won't let me because we'd need a helicopter to get to the nearest hospital.

Eddie

Dear Uncle Morton,

I'm very sorry, but we are leaving your island.

This morning, Mom found another piece of poop in the kitchen. She said that was the final straw.

I did suggest staying here on my own, but Mom said, "Not a chance, buster."

She has already raised the red flag. I just looked through the telescope and saw Mr. McDougall preparing his boat on the mainland. I suppose he'll be here in about fifteen minutes.

I have given all our spare food to the dragons. I have also put some cans on the floor in case they're better at opening them than me.

I will ask Mr. McDougall to come here every day and feed them until you get back.

Eddie

From: Edward Smith-Pickle

To: Morton Pickle

Date: Sunday, February 19

Subject: Sheep

Attachments: The prime suspects

Dear Uncle Morton,

We're still here.

We never left. Mr. McDougall wouldn't let us.

He said the dragons can't stay on your island unsupervised.

Mom asked why not, and Mr. McDougall explained that one of his sheep went missing in the middle of the night. This morning, he found bloodstains on the grass and a trail of wool leading down to the water.

I don't know why he blames your dragons. Arthur can hardly fly and Ziggy can't even leave the house, so there is no way either of them could have gotten from here to the mainland, let alone murdered a sheep. But Mr. McDougall says they are the prime suspects.

Now he has gone home again, and we're stuck here without a key or any food.

Eddie

Dear Eddie,

I am so sorry to hear about your troubles with the front door. I was sure that I had discussed the key with your mother when we talked last week. Has she forgotten our conversation?

This is what I said to her: If you walk down to the end of the garden, you will discover a stone statue of a yellow-headed vulture perched in a shrub. The key is hidden under its left talon.

Please be very careful when you lift it up. That vulture has great sentimental value. It was given to me by the sculptor himself, who lives in a small hut beside the Amazon, and I carried it all the way back from Brazil wrapped in an old shirt.

I have been in touch with Mr. McDougall, who is understandably upset about the loss of his sheep. I assured him that the dragons couldn't be responsible. He didn't appear to be entirely convinced, but I'm sure he'll find the real culprit soon.

All is good here in Ulaanbaatar. I have discovered some fascinating and unexpected information at the National Library, so my visit has already been worthwhile.

The only problem is the weather. Walking the streets without a coat on would be certain death, and even the Reading Room is so cold that no one removes their hats or scarves.

Unfortunately, it's impossible to turn the pages of an old book while wearing gloves, so my fingers are like icicles by the end of the day. Every evening, after leaving the library, I warm myself up at a local restaurant with a bowl of yak stew and a glass of the local brew—a white drink called Airag, made from fermented horse's milk. It tastes better than it sounds.

I'm very sorry about the can opener. Have you looked in the silverware drawer?

With love from your affectionate uncle,

Morton

Dear Uncle Morton,

We found the key!

And we were very careful with the statue.

Mom says you definitely didn't mention it last week. She would have remembered if you had.

You don't have to worry about the can opener. It wasn't in the silverware drawer or anywhere else, but Mr. McDougall's nephew Gordon jetted across this morning in his speedboat and delivered another. He also brought a box of Scottish oat crackers and some delicious cheese.

After he had gone, I found Mom and Emily whispering in the kitchen.

When I asked what was going on, Emily said they were talking about Gordon. Mom thinks he's very handsome.

I don't know if he's handsome, but I like his boat. He said he'll take me for a ride around the island to see the puffins.

Love,

Eddie

From: Edward Smith-Pickle

To: Morton Pickle

Date: Tuesday, February 21

Subject: More sheep

Dear Uncle Morton,

Gordon has been here again. He took us to Lower Bisket in his speedboat to buy food and supplies.

Emily thinks it was a date.

Mom told her not to be ridiculous, but she did turn bright pink.

Apparently, Mr. McDougall is on a rampage. Another sheep went missing last night.

I asked Gordon to tell him that the dragons spent the whole night in my bedroom, with the door shut and the windows locked.

Gordon said I should do the same tonight because Mr. McDougall is planning to stay up from dusk until dawn with a thermos of hot tea and a rifle.

Otherwise, everything is fine. We bought lots of food in the Lower Bisket General Store. The dragons are happy. Even Mom is in a good mood. We went for a walk on the beach this afternoon, and she said it's so peaceful and beautiful she can almost understand why you want to live here.

Eddie

From: Morton Pickle

To: Edward Smith–Pickle

Date: Tuesday, February 21

Subject: Re: More sheep

Dear Eddie,

I have to admit that I am worried by your last message. I know from personal experience that Mr. McDougall is an excellent shot.

On that particular occasion, he wasn't aiming at me, but I should not like to find myself in his sights.

Please make sure that you keep the dragons under observation at all times. I cannot believe that they could be responsible for attacking his livestock, but I wouldn't want to expose them to any unnecessary risks.

I hope your mother enjoyed her date with Gordon. Isn't he a little young for her?

Morton

From: Edward Smith-Pickle

To: Morton Pickle

Date: Wednesday, February 22

Subject: Fish

Attachments: The Fish Museum

Dear Uncle Morton,

You don't have to worry about the dragons. I am keeping a close eye on them.

This morning, I took them for a walk along the beach, and I didn't let them out of my sight for a moment.

I told Mom what you said about Gordon being too young for her, and she said that actually the age difference is only two years and ten months.

Today, Gordon took us to the Fish Museum in Arbothnot. He said it's the biggest attraction in the area.

I suppose it would be very interesting if you like fish.

20

Afterward, Gordon bought us souvenirs at the museum gift shop. He got a plastic shark for me and a marine sticker book for Emily. He wanted to buy a pair of pearl earrings for Mom, but she said they were too expensive, so he got her some smoked salmon instead.

He is coming back tomorrow for tea.

Emily asked if we would have to move to Scotland if they got married. Mom just laughed and said we will cross that bridge when we come to it.

Love,

Eddie

Dear Uncle Morton,

The McDougalls are here.

Mom actually only invited Gordon, but Mr. McDougall came, too.

He won't stop shouting and waving his arms.

He has lost three sheep in a week. Now he wants to take the dragons away and lock them in his barn until the police arrive.

I said he couldn't do that, but he said, "Don't you worry, laddie. It's perfectly legal."

I can't understand how it can be perfectly legal to steal someone else's dragons, but no one is paying any attention to me.

If you get this, please call us ASAP.

Someone has to stop Mr. McDougall!

Eddie

From: Edward Smith-Pickle

To: Morton Pickle

Date: Thursday, February 23

Subject: Your shed

Attachments: The prisoners

Dear Uncle Morton,

The McDougalls have gone.

Everyone argued for a long time, and finally, Mr. McDougall agreed the dragons could stay here as long as they're locked up.

They are now in the shed.

Arthur is miserable. He keeps screaming and wailing and bashing his head against the door, trying to break it open.

I told him he's only in there for his own safety, but he just cried even louder.

Mom says he'll calm down when he's had something to eat. We're going to open a few cans and give the dragons a special supper.

I hope Mr. McDougall catches the sheep thief soon.

Eddie

Dear Uncle Morton,

I'm very sorry, but your dragons have burned down your shed.

Emily and I were having breakfast when we smelled smoke. We ran outside and saw the whole thing blazing.

I put out the fire with buckets of water, but there's not much left except a few black bits of wood.

There's no sign of your dragons, either.

I'm afraid I can't build your shed again. I'm terrible at woodworking. Last time we did it at school, I put a nail through my knee.

But I will find your dragons, I promise.

Eddie

Dear Uncle Morton,

I have discovered who has been eating Mr. McDougall's sheep!

It is the Loch Ness Monster.

I was actually looking for your dragons. I finally found them on the beach, messing around on the sand as if nothing had happened. They didn't even look guilty.

I was just about to give them a piece of my mind when I happened to look out to sea—and I saw this!

I will tell Mr. McDougall as soon as I see him.

Eddie

Dear Eddie,

Thank you for the photo. I'm not an expert, but I would say it's a swan.

Don't worry about Mr. McDougall's sheep or who might be eating them. Keeping the dragons safe is much more important. Could you lock them in the house?

Of course you'll have to let them out every now and then to stretch their wings and go to the bathroom, but please make sure they don't run away again.

The livestock laws are very clear. If Mr. McDougall caught them anywhere near his sheep, he would have a perfect right to shoot them.

My work here is almost done. Last night, I was lucky enough to have dinner with Professor Ganbaataryn Baast, and he has invited me to accompany him on an expedition to the Altai mountains this summer, searching for a famous family of dragons. Apparently, they live in an enormous cave stuffed with gold. No man has ever seen it and lived to tell the tale. Professor Baast intends to be the first—and I shall be the second!

Morton

Dear Uncle Morton,

It is not a swan. It's definitely the Loch Ness Monster. I've got a book about famous mysteries at home and I recognize it from the pictures.

I'm going to search your island for it.

If I get a better photo, I can prove to Mr. McDougall who has really been stealing his sheep, and he'll stop blaming Ziggy and Arthur.

I asked Mom and Emily to help, but they're not interested. They don't even believe I saw the Loch Ness Monster.

In fact, Mom thinks I'm making up stories because of Gordon.

After lunch, she sat me down for a serious talk. She said Gordon isn't her boyfriend, but she might get a boyfriend one day and would I mind?

I said Dad has a new girlfriend every time we see him, so who cares?

Anyway, even if I was upset about Mom having a boyfriend, why would I make up stories about the Loch Ness Monster?

Eddie

Dear Uncle Morton,

I borrowed your boat. I hope you don't mind. I was very careful.

I took the dragons, too. I know you want them to stay locked up, but they'll actually be safer with me. I won't let them out of my sight.

We rowed into the middle of the sea, but there was no sign of the monster.

I would have rowed all the way around the island, but I didn't want to get swept out to sea. So I rowed back to your dock and tied up the boat, then started walking.

I found:

A bird's nest with three eggs.

A whole tree washed up on the beach.

A wrecked boat buried in the sand.

A starfish (dead).

Six crabs (still alive).

Some puffins.

And about a thousand seagulls.

Unfortunately, there was no sign of Nessie.

Do you know of any caves where it might be hiding?

Eddie

Dear Eddie,

Please don't be offended if I say this, but I really don't think you have seen the Loch Ness Monster.

A few years ago, I did a study of the myths and legends surrounding that fabulous beast. I wondered whether it might be a dragon, or a distant relative of the dragon that had somehow become aquatic.

Sadly I discovered that there is no reliable evidence that the monster has ever existed. All the sightings are, I'm afraid to say, the work of maniacs, frauds, fantasists, and publicity seekers of one sort or another.

I wish the monster did exist, but it doesn't. And even if it did, it would be swimming around Loch Ness, not my island.

In the years that I've been living there, I have spotted whales, dolphins, seals, and even the occasional otter, so you may have been lucky enough to see one of them.

I don't know who or what has been stealing Mr. McDougall's sheep, but I can tell you one thing for certain: It is not Nessie.

Morton

If the monster doesn't exist, what's this?

Eddie

From: Morton Pickle

To: Edward Smith-Pickle

Date: Friday, February 24

Subject: Re: Re: Re: Nessie

I'm coming home! Will change my tickets and catch next plane!

Do not approach the monster till I get there! It might be dangerous!

M

From: Edward Smith-Pickle

To: Morton Pickle

Date: Saturday, February 25

Subject: On the beach

Attachments: Flying practice; Air raid

Dear Uncle Morton,

You're right about the monster. It is dangerous. In fact, it's bloodthirsty.

It just tried to eat Arthur.

Ziggy was curled up on the sofa with Emily and Mom, watching some old movie. Arthur and I didn't want to see it, so we went down to the beach again. I was using your binoculars to search for the Loch Ness Monster and Arthur was practicing his flying.

He kept running along the sand and jumping into the air, then flapping his wings to stay up for as long as possible.

I tried to persuade him to land on the beach because rescuing him from the water is no fun at all, but he didn't care.

One time he veered in the wrong direction and headed straight out to sea. I called at him to come back, but he just flew farther and farther from the shore, as if he was trying to get all the way to the mainland.

Suddenly, there was a great burst of water and the monster rose out of the waves, its long neck stretching into the air and its huge mouth opening to reveal two rows of glistening white teeth.

Snap!

It tried to take a bite out of Arthur, but Arthur dodged out of the way just in time.

Snap! Snap!

The monster went for him again and again. Each time Arthur twisted through the air like a fighter pilot. I'd never seen him move so fast.

Finally, he managed to point himself in the right direction and head back to the shore.

The monster charged after him. Both of them were coming straight for me.

Once they reached dry land, the monster couldn't move so quickly. It just waddled up the shore, flapping its flippers on the sand.

Arthur crash-landed at my feet. I could see he was absolutely exhausted by the effort of so much flying. I picked him up and tucked him under my arm, and we ran all the way home.

From now on I'm going to follow your advice. I won't go anywhere near the monster until you get back.

Eddie

Dear Eddie,

I am writing this from Ulaanbaatar airport. The runways are covered in thick snow and slippery ice, so my flight has been delayed. Apparently, we should be boarding within the next hour.

I have to change planes in Moscow and Copenhagen, but if all goes well I should be back in Edinburgh tomorrow morning and home in time for lunch.

I'm glad to hear you're going to keep away from the monster. Perhaps you should stay inside the house until I get back.

Morton

Dear Uncle Morton,

You don't have to come home early if you don't want to.

Everything is fine here now. The monster is gone, and Mr. McDougall has forgiven your dragons.

He wasn't so friendly earlier. He arrived in his rowing boat with Gordon, ready to arrest Ziggy and Arthur.

He had been watching us through his binoculars and saw them snoozing on the grass. He said if we couldn't keep them safely locked up, he would take them straight to the police station in Upper Buckett.

I told him it was actually the Loch Ness Monster who had been stealing his sheep.

He just laughed and said, "Are you sure, laddie? You don't think it's those aliens from outer space?"

I said he should come and see the monster for himself, and he said maybe he would after he arrested the dragons.

He tied a rope around Arthur's neck and marched him down to the boat. Ziggy kept snapping at his legs and blowing little spurts of flames in his direction, but she didn't bite his head off or set him on fire. I suppose she was worried about hurting Arthur, too.

Gordon tried to stop his uncle and so did Mom, but Mr. McDougall wouldn't listen. He said he couldn't afford to lose another sheep and did they want to bankrupt him?

When we got to the dock, Mr. McDougall put Arthur in the bottom of the boat and Ziggy jumped in after them. I tried to climb in, too, but Gordon grabbed me around the middle and said, "Not so fast."

Mr. McDougall dipped his oars and rowed out to sea. We were all shouting at him—me and Emily and Mom and Gordon—but he ignored us. He just headed for the mainland.

The waves got bigger. The boat was rolling around. I was really worried it might tip over and Arthur would drown.

They were almost halfway between the island and the mainland when the monster attacked. It seemed to come from nowhere. It lifted its head out of the water, opened its mouth, and lunged at them.

Mr. McDougall tried to defend himself with one of the oars, but the monster bit the end off. Then it took a big chunk out of the boat.

It would have eaten them all if Ziggy hadn't fought back. She was amazing!

She flapped her wings and lifted herself into the air, then breathed a great big ball of fire straight at the monster's head.

I've never seen anyone look so surprised.

The monster floated there for a moment, its scales smoldering. Then it raised itself out of the waves and struck again.

The battle was terrible. But I always knew who would win. And I was right.

Every time the monster tried to bite Ziggy, she flew out of its way, then turned around and blew back another blazing fireball. Soon, the Loch Ness Monster was black and burnt and smoking from the top of its head to the tip of its tail.

Finally, it plunged under the waves and disappeared in a cloud of bubbles.

Ziggy dragged Arthur and Mr. McDougall back to shore. She couldn't swim very fast with them holding her wings, but that didn't matter. At least they were safe.

Mr. McDougall wasn't very happy about leaving his boat behind, but it was already smashed to pieces and just about to sink.

When they finally got to the beach, Mr. McDougall lay on the sand for a minute or two, getting his breath back. Then he rolled over and said, "I owe you an apology, laddie."

I told him my name is actually Eddie, and he promised to call me that from now on.

He said sorry to the dragons, too.

Now we're all inside your house. I hope you don't mind, but Mr. McDougall has borrowed some of your dry clothes.

Mom is making cocoa for everyone, the dragons
included.

Eddie

Hi E,

I'm changing planes in Moscow.

Just checked timetables and should be home on 3:37 train—could you ask Gordon to meet me?

Glad to hear you're all safe. Please be very careful until I get there. The monster might come back.

M

From: Edward Smith-Pickle

To: Morton Pickle

Date: Sunday, February 26

Subject: Train

Dear Uncle Morton,

You don't have to worry about the monster. I'm sure it won't be coming back.

Even if it does, Ziggy will chase it away again.

Gordon went to meet your train at 3:37, but there was no sign of you. Did you miss your plane?

We have been packing up and getting ready to leave tomorrow.

I'd like to stay on your island for another week, but school starts again on Tuesday, so Mom says we have to go home.

Eddie

From: Edward Smith–Pickle

To: Morton Pickle

Date: Sunday, February 26

Subject: Our last night

 Attachments: The dock; The beach

Dear Uncle Morton,

Gordon got your message about the plane and the train. He will be waiting for you tomorrow morning at 9:01.

Our train leaves at 9:27, so we'll just have time to say hello and good–bye.

We're all packed and ready to go. I'm very sad to be leaving your island, but our last night was awesome. We had a barbecue on the beach—Mr. McDougall, the dragons, Emily, and me.

Mom wasn't there. She went to a restaurant on the mainland with Gordon.

This time it really was a date. Mom was very worried because she hadn't brought any fancy clothes, but Emily and I told her it didn't matter because she looked beautiful just the way she was.

And she did. When she was standing on the dock, waiting for Gordon to pick her up in his speedboat, she looked like someone in a movie.

Once they'd gone, Emily and I collected driftwood on the beach, Ziggy lit the fire, and Mr. McDougall cooked the best barbeque ever.

Mr. McDougall has entirely forgiven your dragons. He says Ziggy is a bonnie lass and she's welcome to as many lamb cutlets as she wants.

The McDougalls have gone home now, but they're coming back to pick us up in the morning.

See you tomorrow!

Eddie

Dear Eddie,

I was so sorry to miss you yesterday. My plane was delayed again, and I finally got to the station at three o'clock in the afternoon. Luckily, Gordon was still waiting for me.

Ziggy and Arthur are both in fine spirits.

They've obviously had a very happy week.
Thank you for looking after them so well.

I brought some presents from Outer Mongolia
to say thank you. I shall send them by first-class
mail.

The McDougalls and I patrolled the shore last
night, armed with torches and shotguns, but the
monster did not return. I do hope she'll come
back soon. I would love to see her for myself.

As you know, Gordon was eager to contact the
newspapers, but I persuaded him not to. For one
thing, I don't want hordes of reporters swarming
across my island. For another, despite her
ferocity, Nessie deserves some privacy.

Apparently Mr. McDougall did tell the whole pub
about her, but everyone just thought he'd had
too many drinks.

We have now agreed she will remain our secret. I
suggest you do the same.

I have not quizzed Gordon on other matters, but I gather he has been in touch with your mother and may be visiting you at some point. Perhaps he could bring the dragons? Or would you like to come and stay again? All of us would be delighted to see you.

Morton

Dear Uncle Morton,

We're back home, too. Our house and our garden feel very small compared to your island, but it's nice to see my stuff again.

I think you're right about keeping quiet about the monster. My book about famous mysteries says Loch Ness is packed with scientists and tourists. You wouldn't want them on your island. In fact, that's probably why she decided to leave Loch Ness in the first place.

I had already shown the photos to Miss Brackenbury, but I've asked her not to tell anyone. She said our secret is safe with her.

Thank you very much for the presents from Outer Mongolia. Emily has been wearing her cashmere scarf nonstop, and I really like my slipper. Please do send the other one if you discover where Arthur hid it.

Mom hasn't tried the Airag yet. She's keeping it for a special occasion.

I talked to Mom about coming back to your island, and she says we'll see. That usually means no, but I think this time it might mean yes.

Love,

Eddie

From: Morton Pickle

To: Edward Smith–Pickle

Date: Wednesday, May 24

Subject: Fwd: One of yours?

Attachments: Clipping

Hi Eddie,

I was sent this by a friend in Australia and thought you might be interested!

M

ADELAIDE DAILY NEWS

Tuesday, May 23rd

Dinosaur Spotted on Popular Adelaide Beach

Swimmers and vacationers were shocked yesterday by the sudden appearance of a mysterious beast on Semaphore Beach.

More than a hundred people fled from the water when an unidentified creature was spotted swimming about twenty meters from the shore.

Reports say that the beast had a small head, a long neck, an enormous brown body, and little flippers.

Some witnesses described it as looking like a dinosaur, leading experts to wonder if a previously unknown species could have been living off the shores of Australia for the past sixty million years.

Beachgoers have been warned to stay out of the water all along Adelaide's beachfront until scientists and experts have studied photographs and footage of the unknown intruder.

No one was hurt and the creature only stayed for a few minutes, leading to speculation that it might have been a trick of the light, a strangely shaped piece of driftwood, or even a great white shark covered in seaweed.

Local resident Gav McPherson remains baffled. "We're used to sharks and sea lions here. Killer jellyfish are no problem, either. But this was something else, mate. I've never seen anything like it."

Police Chief Tina O'Sullivan says her department is keeping an open mind until further investigations have been completed. She refused to comment on speculations that the sighting could be linked to a series of sheep thefts in the area.

What's next for Eddie, Ziggy & Arthur?

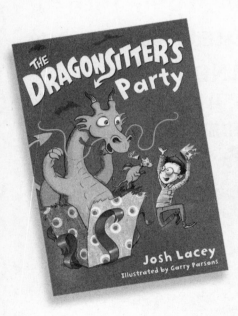

Don't miss their fifth adventure!

Turn the page for a sneak peek.
COMING SOON

ABRACADABRA! KAZAM KAZOOM!!

PREPARE TO BE AMAZED!!!

The world-famous master of magic  Mister Mysterio

will be appearing at Eddie's birthday party

COME AND SEE HIS INCREDIBLE TRICKS

YOU WILL NOT BELIEVE YOUR EYES!

At: Eddie's house

On: Saturday, March 25th   From: 3pm to 5pm

Please RSVP to: Eddie's mom

Dear Uncle Morton,

Did you get my invitation?

I just wanted to check because you're the only person who hasn't RSVPed.

I hope you can come. It's going to be a great party. We're having a magician.

Love from your favorite nephew,

Eddie

Dear Eddie,

I would have loved to come to your party. There is very little that I enjoy more than the work of a good magician.

Unfortunately, I have already promised to stay in Scotland and help on the farm with Mr. McDougall, who is a man short this weekend.

That man is, of course, our mutual friend Gordon, who is very excited about coming to see you. He talks about nothing else.

I can hardly believe that he only met your mother a few weeks ago. He already seems to know much more about her than I do, and I've known her for an entire lifetime.

Mr. McDougall only agreed to give Gordon the weekend off if I would work in his place. It is lambing season here, and the farm has never been busier.

He will be bringing a small birthday surprise for you.

With love from your affectionate uncle,

Morton

Dear Uncle Morton,

Thank you for the surprise. I can't wait to see what it is.

Mom is very excited about Gordon coming to visit. She keeps buying new dresses, then taking them back to the store because they're not quite right.

I'm sorry you can't come to my party. I know my friends would like to meet you. Will you come next year instead?

I'll send you some pictures of Mister Mysterio sawing someone in half.

Apparently that's the best part of his act.

I am going to suggest he pick Emily.

She said, "That's not funny," and I said I wasn't trying to be funny. I just thought the house would be a bit more peaceful if I only had half a sister.

Love,

Eddie

Dear Uncle Morton,

Gordon has arrived with your surprise.

Mom was definitely surprised, but not in a good way.

She said if she'd wanted your dragons to come and stay, she would have invited them.

She was hoping to spend some special time with Gordon this weekend, but she says their time isn't going to be very special if she's got to look after two dragons, not to mention the nineteen kids who will be descending on the house on Saturday afternoon.

Of course, I was very happy to see them.

I can't believe how much Arthur has grown!

He's also getting quite good at flying. We put him in the garden in case he needed to poop after the long drive, and he almost got over the wall.

It's lucky he didn't, because Mrs. Kapelski was pruning her roses and she has a weak heart.

I do wish Ziggy and Arthur could stay for my party. I know my friends would like to meet them.

But Mom said, "Not a chance, buster."

Could you come and get them ASAP?

Love,

Eddie

THE DRAGONSITTER Series

COLLECT THEM ALL!

Be seen with Lola Levine!

MONICA BROWN

LOLA LEVINE IS NOT Mean!

ILLUSTRATED BY Angela Dominguez

MONICA BROWN

LOLA LEVINE Drama Queen

ILLUSTRATED BY Angela Dominguez

MONICA BROWN

LOLA LEVINE and the Ballet Scheme

ILLUSTRATED BY Angela Dominguez

Catch all of Lola's wild adventures in the second grade!

lb-kids.com

SUZANNE SELFORS

THE SASQUATCH ESCAPE

THE IMAGINARY VETERINARY: BOOK 1

SUZANNE SELFORS

THE LONELY LAKE MONSTER

THE IMAGINARY VETERINARY: BOOK 2

SUZANNE SELFORS

THE RAIN DRAGON RESCUE

THE IMAGINARY VETERINARY: BOOK 3

JOIN BEN AND PEARL ON A WILD ADVENTURE THAT'S ANYTHING *BUT* IMAGINARY.

SUZANNE SELFORS

THE ORDER OF THE UNICORN

THE IMAGINARY VETERINARY: BOOK 4

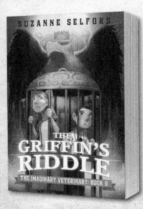

SUZANNE SELFORS

THE GRIFFIN'S RIDDLE

THE IMAGINARY VETERINARY: BOOK 5

SUZANNE SELFORS

THE FAIRY SWARM

THE IMAGINARY VETERINARY: BOOK 6

THE IMAGINARY VETERINARY SERIES

BY SUZANNE SELFORS

  LITTLE, BROWN AND COMPANY
BOOKS FOR YOUNG READERS

lb-kids.com

BC08760

SEE WHERE IT ALL BEGAN!

Find more adventures and play interactive games at
HowToTrainYourDragonSeries.com

  LITTLE, BROWN AND COMPANY
BOOKS FOR YOUNG READERS

BOB740

About the Author

JOSH LACEY is the author of many books for children, including *The Island of Thieves*, *Bearkeeper*, and the Grk series. He worked as a journalist, a teacher, and a screenwriter before writing his first book, *A Dog Called Grk*. Josh lives in London with his wife and daughters.

About the Illustrator

GARRY PARSONS has illustrated several books for children and is the author and illustrator of *Krong!*, winner of the Perth and Kinross Picture Book Award. Garry lives in London.